TRADITIONAL ANIMAL STORIES *of* SOUTH SUDAN

LESSONS FOR ITS CHILDREN

REPENT RITTI JADA

TRADITIONAL ANIMAL STORIES OF SOUTH SUDAN
LESSONS FOR ITS CHILDREN

iUniverse books may be ordered through booksellers or by contacting:

iUniverse
1663 Liberty Drive
Bloomington, IN 47403
www.iuniverse.com
1-800-Authors (1-800-288-4677)

ISBN: 978-1-5320-9564-1 (sc)
ISBN: 978-1-5320-9562-7 (hc)
ISBN: 978-1-5320-9563-4 (e)

Library of Congress Control Number: 2020903206

Print information available on the last page.

iUniverse rev. date: 02/17/2020

CONTENTS

DEDICATION

I AM dedicating this book to the long-suffering children of South Sudan and to their new nation. These young people have known little but war and death during their short lives. But now, with the birth of the world's newest country, they have the opportunity to determine their own destiny.

My fervent prayer is that the lessons these traditional animal stories teach will help to build a peaceful and prosperous South Sudanese society and that all of its citizens will know the best that life has to offer.

ACKNOWLEDGMENTS

I WOULD like to thank my wife, Christiana B. Kamunde, for her constant support and encouragement that enabled me to commit this oral history to paper for the children of South Sudan.

I would also like to remember my dear departed parents for telling me these stories to prepare me for life ahead and helping to educate me in the absence of a school in our village. I would not be where I am today without their love and guidance.

Finally, I would like to thank Dr. Keith D. Martin, a volunteer with Interfaith Works of Montgomery County, Maryland, and an Adjunct Professor at Montgomery College, for working with me over many months to edit these stories.

ABOUT THE AUTHOR

I WAS born in 1962, the fourth of six children, during the first civil war in Sudan, which lasted from 1955 to 1972. I could not start school right away because all the schools in the rural area where I lived were closed during the war.

Fortunately, I was able to begin my education in 1969 by attending Catechism school where we had a Bible class and language instruction two times a week.

I continued my education at the Diko Village Sub/Primary School and then moved to the city of Juba where I graduated from Juba Day Secondary School. From there I received diplomas from Omdurman Ahlia University and Bishop Ngalamu Theological College in Khartoum.

After training with the Civil Aviation Institute, I served in the Fire Department at Juba International Airport and as Staff Sergeant at Khartoum International Airport.

Due to the danger to my family during the

second civil war in Sudan, we fled to Cairo, Egypt, where we were granted refugee status through the UNHCR (United Nations High Commissioner for Refugees) in 2002.

In October of 2003, my wife, three children, and I came to the United States where we have lived ever since. We now have a fourth child who was born in the U.S.

Even though we have now been living in America for more than a decade, I have never forgotten my roots in South Sudan. I am very active in the South Sudanese community in the Washington, DC area, working with an organization called Sudan Sunrise to help build schools in South Sudan.

I hope this book of animal stories will be used in all of South Sudan's schools to teach its children about life and their country's rich cultural heritage.

INTRODUCTION

THESE traditional animal stories are for you, the children of South Sudan, as well as for your parents and everyone else who cares about the future of your country. These stories are your heritage and your path forward as you prepare for your lives ahead.

Perhaps some of these stories have been told to you. They were told to me by my parents when I was growing up in a small Sudanese village with no school. They have been passed down as oral history for generations in the communities of southern Sudan to teach you about what happens in the lives of people. Oral history means that they have never been written down until now.

Over time these stories have changed since they were verbal and not written. Sometimes they have been told in different languages featuring different animals, but they have always been intended to prepare you, the children, for the adult world you will someday inherit.

All of the stories are about struggling and surviving, whether in times of famine, war, migration, political corruption, or relative peace. They are about human beings represented by different animals to make them easier to understand and fun to read. They tell about the good and bad things in life and how to deal with both.

By publishing these stories, I hope they will become a permanent part of the educational process in South Sudan. I also hope they will help you cope with the turmoil your country is currently experiencing. Animals have always been a refuge for all of us as we seek to understand the world around us.

At the end of each story is a brief explanation of what I believe are that story's main lessons. But the lessons I have provided are only one way of thinking about each story. Use your imagination to understand the story in whatever way you would like. There are no right or wrong answers. Seek the lessons that mean something to you.

All the human lessons that the animals in these stories teach are vital to your survival and growth.

You are living in a country where there is often danger, and, like many of the animals in these stories, you need to be very careful. You are the future of your country.

THE QUEEN OF THE
FISH IS SICK

ONCE upon a time, the Queen of the Fish was seriously sick deep in her cave in the water. All the fish were sad and were looking for the best doctor to cure their Queen. The fish were searching over and over in the seas, oceans, and rivers to find out what the problem was with the Queen.

Because the situation of the Queen was getting worse, the senior medical doctor of the sea, Dr. Octopus, recommended Dr. Baboon. "Dr. Baboon has the very best medicine," said Dr. Octopus. Hearing this, the Queen issued orders to all the fish to find Dr. Baboon. So they started searching and kept on searching until they found him. Immediately they told Dr. Baboon about the sickness of the Queen.

Dr. Baboon quickly replied to the fish. "Yes, I know a strong medicine. But it is on the land, and you will have to fight very hard to get it." The fish told him, "We are ready to get the medicine even if it is on the land. We have loyal friends there. We have the power to bring the medicine to the Queen."

Dr. Baboon then told the fish to tell the Queen that she would not survive unless she got a monkey's heart. He said, "I cure many animals with a monkey's heart. It is the best medicine ever found on earth. Once she eats the heart, she will immediately be cured. Please, if you need your Queen to survive, act as soon as possible and let the fish in the rivers, seas, and oceans look for a monkey's heart."

But Dr. Baboon was not telling the truth about the medicine. A monkey's heart would not cure the Queen. The reason he lied was that the baboons were having disputes with the monkeys over the grazing areas. The monkeys were eating the flowers and fruit before they were ripe. So by the time the baboons came, all the food was gone.

The baboons had been trying every trick to get rid of the monkeys. But the monkeys were quick to climb high up on the branches of trees and got away before the baboons could get close to them. Now, by lying to the fish, Dr. Baboon had found a way to destroy his enemy.

Dr. Baboon told the fish how to catch the monkeys in the river during the evening hours. Usually the monkeys came to drink water or eat flowers by the banks of the rivers and often crossed some streams.

"You must be clever to capture these monkeys because they are quick to jump up into the trees, and then you will not be able to catch them. They are small but also the smartest animals on the land. And because they eat day and night, they are very strong," Dr. Baboon said to the fish.

The fish hurried back to tell the Queen of the Fish what Dr. Baboon had said. When she heard his message, the Queen immediately issued an order to all the fish in the rivers, oceans, and seas to kill a monkey so that they could get its heart for her to survive.

The information was supplied to everyone along with strategies on how to get a monkey with its heart. All the big and small fish were mobilized to go and look for the monkeys wherever they were and bring a heart back to the Queen.

It was difficult for the fish to capture a monkey. But one evening a shark was moving near the bank of the river and saw a young monkey eating flowers on the branch of a tree. The shark stopped and said, "Hello, hello," and the monkey turned to the shark and said, "Good evening, Mr. Fish, how can I help you? Do you need some flowers from the trees to eat for supper?"

The shark replied, "No thank you my friend, but I have a question for you. You monkeys live by the river, and we live in the water. So can we be friends and visit each other?"

The monkey answered, "Yes, but how can we do that?" The shark said, "Easily. Today I want you to come with me, meet my family, and see my house, and tomorrow I will go and see where you live."

The monkey replied, "But I don't know how to swim. So how can we get to your house?" The shark said, "It is very simple, Mr. Monkey. You jump on my back and hang onto my fin. I will raise up my back on top of the water until we reach my house. Then I will take you back the same way."

The monkey, who did not know that Dr. Baboon was looking for ways to kill monkeys, believed the shark and agreed to go with him to meet his family and see his house. As the monkey was jumping on the shark's back, a wise mother monkey saw her young friend on the back of the shark.

She screamed, "KO KO KO KO KO," as the shark was moving to the middle of the river. But the monkey did not hear or understand what the mother monkey was shouting.

As soon as the shark was in the middle of the water, the young monkey saw many big and small fish coming around. The monkey began to sense that something was wrong as he was being escorted by thousands of happy fish toward the Queen.

Then the shark said, "Mr. Monkey, do you know that in the world there are good days in life as well as bad days in life? Do you know where we are going?" The monkey replied, "We are going to see your house and family, and hopefully tomorrow you will come and see my family too."

The shark replied, "No, no, no, my friend, that is not the reason. The reason I am taking you now is this: Our Queen has been very ill for a long time, and Dr. Baboon, who lives with you on the land, prescribed your heart as the best medicine to cure our Queen."

"We have been trying to find a monkey's heart for months, and today is a big day in history. I hope you will not be angry as your heart is going to save the Queen of the Fish. All the fish will be happy because our Queen is going to survive right after eating your heart."

The monkey was very sad after hearing what the shark told him. At first, he saw no way to survive. But he still motivated himself and wanted to answer the shark in a wise way that would be beyond the shark's understanding.

After all, he thought, we monkeys survive in the trees, escape from the other animals in the forest, never have a deep sleep, and watch out day and night for danger. It will look stupid for a monkey to die this way. It has never happened in the history of monkeys to be fooled by a shark.

Then the monkey had a brilliant idea. He said to the shark, "Why, my friend, did you not tell me this before? We monkeys are not like the other animals who always have their hearts in them. We leave our hearts in the trees, especially when we come down to eat flowers or drink water. Then we collect our hearts when we go back to sleep. Since it is still early, let us go back, and I will pick up my heart and many more so that the Queen is sure to survive."

The shark stopped and was convinced by what the monkey told him. The shark asked, "Will it be easier for us to get your heart if we go back fast to the place we came from?" The monkey said, "Sure. Then not only can I get my heart, but I can collect many more hearts because I know where all the monkeys keep their hearts."

The shark quickly turned around and started going back. As soon as the fish who were escorting the monkey to the Queen saw this, they cried out, "He's lying." The shark was trying to listen, but the monkey, who now believed he could save himself, kept shouting to the shark to go quickly since it was getting late and dark.

The fish swam faster and faster to tell the shark that one time they had seen the dead body of a monkey with its heart still in it. The shark paid no attention, and the monkey breathed a sigh of relief.

Soon the shark and the monkey reached the shore of the river. As the monkey was about to jump off, some of the stronger fish leapt way out of the water to tell the shark not to let the monkey touch the trees. But they were too late. The monkey had already jumped very quickly to catch a branch of the tree and without even looking back climbed up to the highest branch.

Then the monkey turned back and said to the shark, "You are very stupid, Mr. Shark. Do you think any animal in this world can live with its heart outside of itself ? Go back and tell your Queen that Dr. Baboon betrayed me. If you need a heart, then take Dr. Baboon's heart because you will not get mine. You will not see me again. Please go and don't waste your time."

From there the monkey went and called an emergency meeting and told the other monkeys, "The enemy who betrayed us is Dr. Baboon, our neighbor."

What happened next? The Queen of the Fish, who was willing to kill a monkey to save herself, died. The monkeys demanded that the baboons stop trying to kill them. In return, the monkeys agreed not to eat all the food in the grazing areas. The two animal groups signed a treaty and lived together in peace ever after.

* * * * *

In this story, an innocent young monkey trusts someone without knowing much about him. As a result, he finds himself tricked into a critical situation where his life is in danger. Three major lessons can be learned here.

First, be sure you know all about the people you choose to associate with because even your neighbors can betray you.

Second, if you fail to do this, don't give up because you still have the ability to use your brain to figure out how to escape from danger.

Third, if you are having a conflict with someone, try to resolve your differences so you can live in peace just as the baboons and monkeys did.

ANIMALS REVOLT AGAINST MEN AND WOMEN FOR THE FIRST TIME

ONCE upon a time, men, women, and all the animals of the forest were living together in harmony. Cats and dogs were the closest friends and messengers to the men and women. The cats and dogs understood human language better than the other animals. The men and women preferred to have the cats and dogs close to them because of their loyalty.

Among the animals, the hyena was very active. She got up early in the morning to hunt other animals in secret to provide extra food for her family. Because the hyena also gave some bones and a small amount of meat to the cats and dogs, they appreciated the hyena's attitude toward them. They liked the hyena but didn't tell this to the other animals.

One time after returning from hunting, the hyena asked the cats and dogs to tell her what the men and women were saying when they sat together. "Usually when they are talking they point to the animals and birds. I try hard to read their faces, but I still don't know what they are saying," the hyena said. "Please tell me what they are talking about since you understand the language better."

The cats and dogs looked at each other but did not reply to the hyena because they heard all the human's plans and were advised not to tell the other animals anything.

That silence made the hyena suspicious that something was wrong. She became serious and said, "I will no longer bring you the meat and bones as before unless you reveal to me the secret you know and why you have refused to tell it to me."

But still, the cats and dogs did not answer. Again, the hyena warned them, "Unless you tell me about the meetings of the men and women, I will not give you your share of the bones and meat."

Because the cats and dogs were hungry and needed food for their families, they told the hyena about the people's secret plot against the animals. All animals that are not loyal to the men and women are to be dealt with as follows:

1. No longer can any animal come near to their table while they are eating. Now the men and women will put a distance between themselves and all the animals.
2. Some animals will be slaughtered to be food for the men and women.
3. The big animals will be tied down for the use of the men and women.

4. There will be no freedom for the animals to come and go on their own.

5. Some strong animals will provide transportation.

6. Other animal groups will bring water and some will be used for milk and cultivation.

7. The animals will be given only a limited time to eat.

8. Some animals will be used for protection.

The cats and dogs told the hyena that the humans had agreed to use the animals in these ways for their entire lives. The men and women had also agreed to start tying down the aggressive and strong animals that very night to begin this new era.

If any animals resisted, they and their leaders were to be immediately killed. The men and women believed this would bring stability and forever establish a difference between animals and human beings.

Furthermore, according to the cats and dogs, the hyena was specifically mentioned by name at the meetings as one of the notorious animals that proclaimed animal rights and wanted to make animals equal to men and women.

The hyena was worried as she heard this agenda and quickly gave the bones and meat to the dogs and cats. Then she ran to mobilize all the animals to come to an emergency meeting that evening.

During the meeting the hyena explained the situation to the leaders of all the different kinds of animals. The hyena told them that the men and women will put an end to animal development and freedom, and this will be the worst thing ever to happen in animal history.

The animals understood everything very clearly. Then the hyena said, "We animals must be out of here now, away from the men and women, before they begin to implement their plan. Remember, the big and strong animals are to protect the smaller ones. The lions and elephants are to threaten the men and women, so everyone will have time to escape to freedom, safety, and happiness."

At the end of the meeting the lion said he would let out a loud roar at the time of the evacuation. All the other animals yelled that they would cry out to confuse the men and women. The zebra added, "My stripes will confuse them even more."

The elephant promised to destroy the fence so all the animals, big and small, could escape. "We big animals have to open the way for all the animals," the elephant said.

When the time came, the animals put the revolution into action, trampling over the destroyed fence that lay on the ground. The men and women were confused by all the shouting, the destruction of the fence, and the big tree limbs lying everywhere that the giraffe had pulled down. They did not know what was happening until morning when some of the animals came back to be loyal to the men and women.

After three days, the hyena took some strong animals as her body guards and returned to see if any of the animals that had come back wanted to escape now. It was worse than the hyena had thought. She discovered that the men and women had already implemented their plan. Most of the animals were tied up inside the barn and could not come out.

When the hyena saw this, she spoke to them, "My brothers and sisters, I told you, but you did not listen. I tried to free you from slavery, but it seems you enjoy being slaves to these men and women. Even though you decided to come back, you are still welcome to the everlasting freedom in the forest. But if you enjoy it here then stay." With that the hyena left.

A month later the hyena came back again to check on the captive animals. The donkey cried out from inside the fence, "I want to escape, but I cannot because of this strong fence. Tell my friends that live with you in freedom that I have to take water to the homes of all the men and women, but they have yet to pay me for this hard work."

The hyena said, "Thank you for telling me what your life is like in captivity. Enjoy what you deserve." Then she returned to the forest and did not come back again. This is why, today, some animals are wild and free while others still live with men and women and do whatever they are told to do by their human masters.

* * * * *

This is a story about human nature and the desire of people to put others down so they can be on top. In society this often leads to unfairness. In this story the men and women decided that they wanted all the power.

This story also shows that it is possible to create a more equal society as the wild animals did. Sometimes you have a choice and sometimes, because of a dangerous situation, you may not be able to do what you want to do right away.

Whatever your situation, live your life the best way you can and keep looking for opportunities to achieve your dreams.

THE RABBIT WHO
WANTS TO BE KING

ONCE upon a time, the entire universe was ruled by one King who lived in space watching over heaven and earth. One day, he decided that the earth and its animals should be ruled separately from the heaven and its animals.

So he invited all the animals from earth to come up into space to compete to become King of Earth.

There was just one problem. The invitation stated that only those animals who could fly to heaven could participate. And most of the animals who wanted to go didn't have wings.

Even some of the birds couldn't make the trip because they had a maximum flying time of only a few hours. Getting to heaven would take at least twelve hours without rest. Only the fastest and strongest flyers would succeed.

Tension became very high between the animals with wings and the animals without wings. Some even asked the King to come to earth for the selection. But the King would not change his mind. He said, "If you are not able to come, you are not fit to be the King of Earth."

After the King made his ruling, a clever animal called Mr. Rabbit announced that he wanted to be named King of Earth. All the other animals wondered how this was going to happen if Mr. Rabbit couldn't fly. He could only run a short distance before he got tired. And he didn't even have wings, so how could he fly?

The other animals just laughed. "Is he kidding?" they asked. But Mr. Rabbit was serious. He said he would fly and compete.

As the day for departing to heaven approached, Mr. Rabbit went to see Mr. Bugle, one of earth's strongest birds. "Mr. Bugle," he said, "I will arrange your luggage for the flight. You go home and rest before your long flight to heaven."

Mr. Bugle was grateful for Mr. Rabbit's assistance and gladly went home to bed. But while Mr. Bugle was sleeping, the clever rabbit took everything out of the bird's luggage and crawled in.

When the time came to leave, Mr. Bugle strapped his luggage on his back and joined the other birds who were ready to fly. Off they all went. After twelve hours, Mr. Bugle reached heaven. But he did not know that Mr. Rabbit was in his luggage.

Unfortunately, not all the birds made it to heaven. About halfway through their journey, they began complaining that their bags were much heavier than when they had packed them the night before the flight. Many of the weaker birds started to fall back to earth. Some even died in the air.

Why did this happen? Mr. Rabbit had played yet

another trick. Just before crawling into Mr. Bugle's luggage, Mr. Rabbit snuck into the homes of all the other birds and secretly put stones in their bags. The clever rabbit did this to stop as many animals as possible from reaching heaven to compete with him to be the King of Earth.

All the birds who did make it to heaven were very proud of themselves. They were also proud that they had left Mr. Rabbit on earth. Now was the time for a bird to be King over all the animals on earth. But just as they were speaking of their victory, Mr. Rabbit popped out of Mr. Bugle's bag. This made Mr. Bugle very ashamed and angry, but there was nothing he could do.

Soon the time came for the King and his Cabinet Ministers to arrive. They were very well dressed. Most of the big birds, including the bugle, didn't have their best clothes with them because the clever rabbit had taken them out of their luggage.

Mr. Rabbit, however, was wearing his professional clothes. When he addressed the King and his Cabinet Ministers, they were all very impressed. The King quickly ruled that the clever rabbit should be the King of all the animals on earth.

He immediately crowned Mr. Rabbit, who then spoke to his new subjects, "Today I am your King, and there will be peace in heaven and on earth." This made all the birds very angry. They did not accept him as their King. After the rabbit's speech, the birds checked their bags one by one to make sure that he would be left forever in heaven.

"How can he rule the animals on earth from heaven?" said the bugle bird. Mr. Rabbit was looking at the birds as they checked their bags. He asked some birds to do him a favor and bring him home, but not one bird agreed to take him down to earth.

Instead, the birds left him in heaven and carried back the message that Mr. Rabbit was not a real King. "Let's see how he will rule us from heaven," all the birds said. "It is a twelve-hour flight and not possible for him to come again to earth."

After the birds left, King Rabbit requested an emergency meeting with the King of Heaven and his Cabinet Ministers. He thanked them for choosing him to be King over the animals on earth. King Rabbit stressed the need for all the animals in heaven and on earth to cooperate and build strategies for peaceful relations.

"I decided to stay back here to express my gratitude to you for selecting me to be King of Earth," said King Rabbit. "Your Excellency the King of Heaven, Cabinet Ministers, and Distinguished Animals of Heaven, on behalf of all the animals on earth, I want to thank you for the excellent job you have done for us."

"Our relationship is going to be forever and ever," he continued. "We animals on earth have many resources of all kinds both for you and for us. Every year I will invite your King and his Cabinet Ministers to visit earth. I will send my powerful birds to come and carry you to earth and bring you all back to heaven."

As King Rabbit was saying this, all the animals in heaven were so happy and cried out, "We salute you King Rabbit." Then King Rabbit said, "If you do me a favor, I will promise you something you have never seen before." Everyone said, "We will do whatever you want us to do for you."

King Rabbit responded. "Collect as many ropes as you can. Connect them to each other and tie me in a bag with food. Then lower the bag down to earth. As soon as I reach land, I will order my people to tie the best gift of all for you in heaven. It is a gift you have never seen before in your lives. You will have it within a few hours of my arrival."

The heaven animals rejoiced again. They immediately started collecting ropes and connecting them together to form one long rope. After they had finished doing this, they attached a bag to one end of the rope.

Finally, King Rabbit asked the animals to tie him into the sack. "Hold onto the rope until I safely reach earth," he instructed them from inside the bag. "Then wait until my guards tug the rope three times. After that, pull up the rope to receive the gift I have promised. You will enjoy it forever."

King Rabbit landed on earth safely. He was welcomed by the animals, who were surprised to see him. He told them that the animals in heaven urgently needed stones and rocks because they did not have any.

The animals on earth believed him and quickly tied stones and rocks to the rope. Then King Rabbit's guards tugged the rope three times. The animals in heaven felt the tug and pulled up the rope. But as soon as the gift reached heaven, they realized that King Rabbit had deceived them.

Stones and rocks were not the best gift of all. Enraged, they decided to throw everything back down to earth to kill King Rabbit and all the other animals with him.

Guessing this would happen, King Rabbit quickly asked his enemies to wait where the rope was. He said that the animals in heaven had promised to send down gifts for those animals who still opposed him. At the same time, King Rabbit told those who supported him to go home right away and come back tomorrow for a meeting.

As soon as King Rabbit went away with all his supporters, the stones and rocks from heaven started falling. None of the animals who had disagreed with him survived, and the relationship between the animals in heaven and on earth was permanently disconnected.

King Rabbit continued to rule his Kingdom for many years without opposition until his death at the hands of the animals with two legs living in a house.

* * * * *

This story describes how the desire for power can make someone act in a bad way. The rabbit represents a clever person who wants to become the ruler of everyone and everything.

He develops a deceptive strategy to become King that ends up harming or killing his competitors. Then to remain in power, he uses even more violence. It is important to be aware of what leaders are doing and the motivations behind their actions.

IV

THE ELEPHANT KING
FINDS A WISE HUSBAND
FOR HIS DAUGHTER

ONCE upon a time, there was an elephant who was King of all the animals. He had a daughter who grew up to become the most beautiful female elephant in the Kingdom. When the time came for his daughter to get married, the King wanted her to marry the wisest animal in his Kingdom.

The King proclaimed, "If any animal can bring me what I want, I will give my daughter to him. I will have a big festival and invite all the animals to come and celebrate. I need only one grown-up beautiful cow, neither male nor female, to be paid to me as a dowry for my daughter. I will divide this nation equally with whomever brings me this cow."

Every animal, from the biggest to the smallest, tried to find the dowry that the King wanted. But none of them could, not even the lion, leopard, or any other of the big and powerful animals. When all these animals had failed, the bat, who was hanging upside down on a tree, said, "This is now my time to come down to get married to the King's daughter." All the animals laughed, "HA HA HA HA," when they heard what the bat said. "Mr. Bat, you are without a house for yourself, and you only have enough food for yourself. How can you give the dowry to the King?"

Mr. Bat ignored them and cried out to the King, "I am ready to marry your daughter, and I am able to provide the dowry to you tomorrow morning. I will give you exactly what you want, and you will be happy with it." The King thought for a while and said, 'Mr. Bat, are you sure?"

The bat replied, "Sir, I have the cow, neither male nor female as you said, for your daughter's marriage. It is ready. Please send your servants to my house to bring it to your palace. But, Sir Mr. King, don't send your servants during day time or night time."

The King paused to think about what the bat had said. Then Mr. Bat repeated, "Send your servants to get your cow but not during the day or night." The King got up, and all the animals kept quiet as they waited for his reply. "Mr. Bat," said the King, "where do you get such wisdom? You have solved the riddle, and from today on and forever my daughter will be your wife. I will divide this nation with you because of your knowledge."

The King told his servants and all the animals to prepare for the marriage ceremony. The animals heard the King's promise to Mr. Bat. They celebrated, and so began the marriage festival that lasted for seven days and seven nights with eating, dancing, singing, and playing games.

Everyone was happy about the marriage of the King's beautiful daughter to Mr. Bat, who was the wisest animal of them all.

* * * * *

The lesson of this story is that it is better to marry a wise person rather than someone who is rich, greedy, or selfish. Knowledge and wisdom are the keys to success and happiness.

V

THE ISLAND OF PEACE
TURNS VIOLENT

ONCE upon a time, there was a kind and loving Chief named Gowrie who wanted all the animals to live together in harmony on the Island of Peace. The island had two big beautiful mountains with tall trees and a large lake with swamps, fertile land, and all kinds of food. The area was quiet, with only the Chief's guards watching in case anything happened to disturb the peace.

Unfortunately, because of their happiness, most of the animals were getting lazy. They didn't want to build homes for themselves. They only wanted to enjoy the opportunities given to them by the Chief. Many of them even started acting crazy and turned against their friends.

Some animals began feeding on other animals. Some reptiles fed on other reptiles. Some snakes ate baby birds and bird eggs. Wild birds devoured other birds and small animals. The Island of Peace was turning into an island of violence.

The Chief realized that there were serious problems on the island. He got angry and warned the animals to stop mistreating each other. But they did not listen. So the Chief decided to evict all the animals from the island whether they liked it or not.

"This island was meant for peace, not for violence," proclaimed the Chief. "In one year, during the dry season, I will burn the entire island." This was his final warning to all the animals living there.

This was terrible news for the animals. The smaller animals and those who felt threatened started to leave immediately. But most of the animals who had been born in the middle of the violence never knew peace and didn't believe the Chief. They started acting worse than before, threatening more animals and even the Chief 's guards.

The final day came in the middle of February a year later. It was windy and hot. All the leaves were dried up, and the Chief supplied his guards with matches. Soon the fire was everywhere on the island. The animals now realized that what the Chief had said was true.

Although the Chief had originally only wanted to evict the animals, now he planned to kill them because they had not heeded his warnings. Thousands of animals died in minutes. No place on the island was safe. Birds fell from the sky. In the mountains, animals burned in their caves. Fish were boiled alive in the lake. Reptiles in the swamps stopped breathing.

While all this was happening, there was a snake who was trying to survive. He begged a big bird who was flying nearby to save him. "Please Ms. Bird, I am so helpless that I really need you to rescue me. Can I just roll on your neck, so you can take me out of this fire to a safe place?" Then the snake started to cry.

The big bird took pity on the snake. She agreed to fly him out of the hot fire and land him in a safe area. The snake was happy to have arranged his escape. The snake also had another thought about what he would do once the bird landed him safely.

As soon as they touched the ground, the snake refused to get off the bird. Instead, he rolled on more tightly. Then the snake said, "Because of the fire I have not eaten since yesterday, and I am very hungry. If I let you go, I will have no supper today."

The big bird was sad and regretted helping the snake. She wished that she had never talked to him or even looked at him. But then, she quickly stopped thinking this way and immediately made a new plan to survive. "Mr. Snake," said the bird, "I saw the smoke of the fire coming directly toward us. If you want to survive, let me take you farther away where you will be completely safe from death." The snake agreed right away because he was so hungry.

The bird told the snake to leave her neck and roll onto her leg so that she could fly up really fast and land somewhere safer. The snake did what he was told and rolled onto the bird's leg.

The bird took off into the air directly into the hot smoke of the fire. The snake said, "Hey Ms. Bird, turn left, turn right, turn around." But the bird kept flying into the fire. The snake cried, "No bird, no bird, no bird." Ms. Bird flew right through the hot smoke of the fire, straightened her leg, uncurled her toes, dropped the snake into the fire, and quickly flew very far away.

That was the last relationship between snakes and birds. And it was the end of the Island of Peace.

* * * * *

When someone helps you, you must thank them and be grateful. If you turn against that person, you may become the victim like the snake. And if you are the one who helps another, you must be smart to make sure you are not betrayed.

VI

A CAT TRIES TO MAKE
A DONKEY BEHAVE

ONCE upon a time, a farmer had a donkey, cat, chicken, goat, and cow. The one closest to the farmer was the cat. They all behaved well except the donkey. Every time the donkey ate he would fall down and thrash his legs about in a wild way.

The cat saw that this type of behavior was not good and could be dangerous because the donkey might kick the other animals and hurt them.

So the cat went to the donkey and said, "Hi, Mr. Donkey, please don't throw your legs that way. It is not good behavior when you are living with others." The donkey replied, "Hey, Ms. Cat, you are bothering me. Go away from here with your nonsense."

Next the cat went to the chicken and told the chicken that the donkey's behavior was not good. The cat asked the chicken to tell the donkey to stop kicking his legs about, but the chicken replied, "Stupid cat, go away. You are bothering me. It is none of your business what the donkey does."

Then the cat went to the goat and gave the goat the same message. The goat replied, "Mind your own business and leave the donkey alone." Finally, the cat talked to the cow. The cow said, "I am not concerned about what the donkey is doing. I have nothing to do with him. Get away from here." After that the cat went back to her place and sat down to see what would happen.

A few weeks later the donkey was eating as usual and was happily thrashing his legs about. At the same time the farmer came by with his small boy. The donkey's legs hit the child, seriously injuring him.

Because the farmer had no transportation, he hitched his wagon to the donkey to take his son to the hospital. To make the donkey go faster, the farmer sat on him and hit the donkey hard on his sides. Sadly, the child died before they got to the hospital.

When the farmer got back home he began preparations for a big funeral. The donkey was still bleeding badly from being hit so often on the way to the hospital. But the farmer made the donkey pull the wagon again to bring chairs, water, and food for the funeral. And since there were so many guests, there wasn't enough food. So the farmer took the cow, goat, and chicken to be slaughtered.

The cat, who was sitting by the side of the house, asked the donkey what had happened. The donkey said, "If I had listened to you before, none of these awful things would have happened. Now the farmer's son, the cow, goat, and chicken are dead, and I am seriously hurt."

The cat replied, "You insulted me and so did the cow, goat, and chicken. None of you did anything to solve the problem and because of that it became a tragedy." The donkey was very sorry. He apologized to the cat and proclaimed, "You are a prophet!"

* * * * *

This story has a real hero: The cat. She saw a problem and did everything she could to solve it even though it was not her problem. Because everyone was very selfish and did not care, the situation got much, much worse. The lesson here is that if you see a problem and can do something about it without endangering yourself, then you must do the right thing.

VII

ALL THE ANIMALS ARE
WITHOUT TAILS

ONCE upon a time, all the animals were without tails. For this reason, they faced many problems, especially in the grazing areas where the mosquitoes were biting. They had no tails to swat these flies away. The animals complained and complained and asked the King of the animals to solve this problem.

The King thought it was a good idea for him to help his subjects. He immediately called a meeting of the animal leaders to fix this problem. At the meeting they decided to gather all the animals together and distribute tails to each of them. The King and the animal leaders decided on the different types of tails for all the animals on earth.

When the King announced the date and time for distributing the tails, his message was clear: "The tails are free for all animals. But after the date of distribution of the tails, no more tails will be given to anyone. If some animals refuse a tail and later want one, they have only themselves to blame."

The King added, "The only animals that will not be included are men and women because before we escaped to live freely in the forest, they used us as tools to work for them. Let no animal reveal this secret to the humans. Otherwise, they will not allow us to have tails and will force us to live in everlasting suffering."

When the day came, the animals started to gather. The King arrived with his soldiers and Cabinet Ministers. After welcoming all who came, the King ordered the distribution of the tails.

Right away all the animals who chose to receive tails were very happy. Now they could swat all the mosquitoes and not get bitten anymore. They were thankful for this great gift from their King.

However, some animals refused to accept tails. They opposed the idea of having a tail because this had never happened before. For example, the chimpanzees, who lived in the caves of the mountains, thought that only their ideas were good. The tails were bad because the idea was not their own.

Sadly, because they did not receive tails, the chimps became mostly isolated from the other animals all over the world. Now, when the chimps appeared, the other animals were afraid to come near them because without tails, the chimps resembled men and women.

This situation made the chimps very unhappy, and they finally decided to go to the King to ask for tails. But the King told them it was too late.

They made up excuses and pleaded with the King, but he did not listen. So the chimps returned to their caves in sorrow.

That is why to this day, chimpanzees remain without tails while other animals have them.

* * * * *

Do not be afraid of new ideas. When presented with a good opportunity, such as the chimps were, it is important to listen. If you refuse to be open to what is new, you risk becoming isolated and missing out on the chance to improve your life.

VIII

TWO FRIENDS PLOT
AGAINST AN ELEPHANT

ONCE upon a time, two animals called Mr. Turtle and Ms. Rabbit were best friends. One day Ms. Rabbit came up with an idea to share with Mr. Turtle. "Look," she said to Mr. Turtle, "all the other animals are much stronger than we are. Why is that? Do you know anything we can do to help us get strong?"

Mr. Turtle said he had no idea. Ms. Rabbit replied that they had to make their brains work extra hard to find a way to get fresh meat. "Meat," she said, "will make us strong and run faster than the other animals. The best meat is elephant meat. It will make us strong and big like him. To stay alive we need elephant meat."

Mr. Turtle asked how they could do this since the elephant was one of the biggest and strongest animals on earth. Other animals feared him. No animal could kill him, certainly not animals as small as a rabbit and a turtle.

The rabbit said, "We have to play a very dirty game to stay alive. And I know just the game because I am the master mind for all the animals living in the forest, including the elephant. I will show you how that big animal will give his body for us to eat as meat." "I don't believe you," the turtle said.

So the rabbit explained that in a world where everyone is without eyes, the animal with one eye is King because he is the only one who can see what is happening. Mr. Turtle was very confused by this. "But big animals like the elephant have two eyes," he said. "They also have bigger brains than small animals."

Ms. Rabbit disagreed. "Big animals don't have bigger brains because they are never in danger. They are just happy to eat, drink, and sleep. They don't worry about other animals killing them."

"But smaller animals always worry about surviving and are always ready to run at any time. Smaller animals have many more enemies than big animals. All the time they are thinking about themselves and their children being safe. Because of this, small animals have bigger brains than big animals," Ms. Rabbit said.

Mr. Turtle finally understood the rabbit's point. But he was still completely confused about how they could get the elephant to give them his meat.

Ms. Rabbit laughed, "HA HA HA HA. You know, my friend, first we will get into his brain and confuse him. He will no longer be able to think clearly. Whatever we say he will agree with."

Ms. Rabbit continued to explain her strategy. "What elephants fear most is death. So we are going to convince him that he is dying. You will do your part, and I will do mine."

"Tomorrow I will go to Mr. Elephant and tell him that the Witch Doctor prophesized that he will die soon if he does not take the Witch Doctor's medicine. At this point the elephant will become afraid and confused. It will be difficult for him to think correctly."

"He will humbly start to find out how he can survive and what treatment he needs. Then you will come along with some options and solutions to calm him down. He will say yes to everything you suggest until he dies."

"Now," said Ms. Rabbit, "I am going to make an appointment with him to meet you under the big tree. You will pretend to be the Witch Doctor and explain his sickness to him. You will put it directly to him that if he does not respect you, he is surely going to die. But before you come, I am going to tell him you are a great doctor who has cured many animals in the forest."

"I will also tell him," Ms. Rabbit added, "that the Witch Doctor said he must close his eyes and open his trunk really wide, so the doctor can put the medicine in. He must not reopen his eyes or close his trunk until the doctor says OK. He must obey these instructions or he will die."

"Then, when he opens his trunk, I will climb into his stomach with two buckets, one for you and one for me. I will get as much fresh elephant meat as I can."

"After I come out and go away with the buckets full of meat, you will tell the elephant to open his eyes, close his trunk, and rest for some time. Then you must quickly leave and join me at my house."

The two animals ran off to find Mr. Elephant and implement Ms. Rabbit's strategy. They did it successfully again and again. After each time, the rabbit told the turtle to come to her house to get his share of the meat from the elephant's stomach.

But before the turtle came to the rabbit's home, she hid most of the meat and gave very little to the turtle. Ms. Rabbit explained away the small portion, saying that wild animals attacked her on her way home and stole most of the meat.

The turtle was not happy with the amount of meat he was receiving. So he decided to secretly send Ms. Fox to the rabbit's home to find out if what the rabbit was saying was true. Ms. Fox learned from the rabbit's children that their mommy brought the meat from the elephant's stomach and hid most of it in the house.

Ms. Fox told this to Mr. Turtle. Somehow this message also reached the elephant. But neither Ms. Rabbit nor Mr. Turtle knew this had happened. The next time the turtle and the rabbit came to take some meat from the elephant, he had all the information about the plan of the two small animals.

After Ms. Rabbit had crawled into the elephant's stomach, the elephant caught the turtle and put him under one of his big feet. Then the elephant closed his trunk with the rabbit still inside and told the turtle, "I know what you and the rabbit have been doing."

The turtle was very afraid and said, "It was her idea to take your meat for fresh food." The rabbit heard this from inside the elephant's stomach and knew that she and the turtle were in great danger. She warned the elephant to open his trunk. If not, she said, she would immediately cut out his heart.

At the same time the rabbit was issuing this warning, the elephant decided to crush the turtle and destroy him completely. After that, the elephant planned to release and catch the rabbit and throw her against a big tree.

The rabbit realized she had to act immediately. So before the elephant had time to lift up his foot and bring it down to crush the turtle, Ms. Rabbit cut out the elephant's heart with a knife. Immediately he fell over and died.

Even though he was angry at Ms. Rabbit for cheating him out of his fair share of the meat, Mr. Turtle helped her escape from the elephant's stomach. Then the two animals ran away with their last buckets of elephant meat and were never friends again.

* * * * *

We live in a world where smart people sometimes have secret plans to hurt and even kill other people. In this story, the rabbit and turtle plot to destroy an innocent elephant just so they can get his meat. Then the rabbit betrays the turtle by keeping more than her fair share of the meat.

Remember, just because someone is clever, this does not necessarily mean that he or she is a good person.

IX

AN ANIMAL CONFERENCE DETERMINES THE WISEST ANIMAL

O NCE upon a time, there was a debate about which animals were the smartest and wisest on earth and why they were so clever. It was decided that a conference was necessary to settle this question. An invitation was sent across the earth to all the animal groups, including reptiles, fish, birds, and those that lived on the land. The conference was held on one of the biggest islands. All the animals attended.

Each group of animals proclaimed itself to be the wisest and, therefore, the boss of everyone. The biggest animals, including the elephants, claimed the title because they were the strongest. But the smallest animals said that strength did not bring wisdom.

The reptiles and fish said they were the smartest because they ruled the rivers, lakes, and oceans. The land animals said no. The birds argued that since they were the eyes of the earth flying everywhere, they knew more than anyone. Everyone else disagreed with them.

Then a man and woman came forward. They said they controlled the earth, and that meant they were the wisest. Nearly all the animals agreed with them.

Only two animals, a cat and a dog, refused to honor the man and woman. The cat and dog said they would agree with all the other animals that men and women were the smartest only if the animals answered "Yes" to one question.

Hearing this, the other animals became split in

their opinions. Some of them said, "Please don't waste your time with such kinds of animals as the dog and cat." But others said, "Let them ask their question." Finally, the lion cried out with a high and angry voice, "Don't listen to this silly question because men and women are the boss on earth."

The cat replied, "Listen you stupid animals. You said men and women are the smartest. But did you know they are our servants? They wash our bodies clean and feed us. They pet and love us. They let us live in their homes. We can even jump on them. So, here is the question: Can any of you use men and women in this way?"

Every animal said "No." "Some of us may be very strong or big," said the lion on behalf of all the animals, "but we cannot make men and women do these things for us. We must admit that the cat and dog are really the smartest animals living on earth because men and women respect them so much."

Then all the animals returned to their homes with sadness because they knew they were not the smartest.

* * * * *

When living with someone who is more powerful than you are, you must be wise and smart. If you are, then the powerful ones will most likely end up taking care of you, just like the human beings did for the cats and dogs in this story.

A COURT CASE ABOUT A
MALE AND FEMALE COW

ONCE upon a time, a lion and a hyena were neighbors. Because the lion was bigger and stronger, he used the hyena as his servant to clean his house. The lion demanded that the hyena take away the bones of the animals that the lion had eaten because they attracted flies. Usually after the hyena finished her work, the lion would give her some leftovers of skin and bones. Then the hyena went back home.

The hyena was small, but she had many cows, both female and male. One day as the lion was coming home from hunting, he passed by the hyena's home and saw all her cows. The lion did not expect the hyena to have so many cows. He became envious of her and got an idea.

He called the hyena and told her that when he and his wife went hunting, their only cow was alone at home. The lion asked the hyena, "Would you allow me to bring my cow to stay with your cows until I come and take him back?"

Not knowing that the lion had bad intentions against her cows, the hyena replied, "Yes, you may bring your male cow and take him back at any time. I will keep him with my cows inside the fence here."

After a short period of time, one of the hyena's female cows gave birth to two calves. When the lion heard of the birth, he went to the hyena and asked her, "When did my cow give birth to twin calves?" The hyena replied, "Sir, your cow is a male cow, and I kept only one cow for you. It was my female cow that gave birth, not your cow."

The lion got very angry. He said it was his male cow that gave birth, and he wanted to take his cow with the two calves home with him. The hyena tried to reason with him, but the lion said, "Do you want me to use force, Ms. Hyena? If you want to dispute my rights, I will use force now."

The hyena was afraid of the lion and said, "Sir, let us look for a legal procedure to determine whether it is your cow or mine that gave birth. If the calves are legally yours, then you may take them. If the calves are mine, the legal people will give them to me." The lion said, "Yes, yes, let us go to Court."

The hyena went to the Chief of the animals and explained the situation. The Chief called for the Emergency Court of Appeals to hear the case and invited all the animals to attend the Court. The Chief set the day and time for the Court, and all the animals came except the rabbit.

The hearing started, and the Chief of the animals asked the hyena to explain what had happened. The hyena testified that the lion claimed that his male cow was the one who had given birth to the twin calves. The hyena added that this was impossible because only female cows can give birth.

The lion was asked to respond, but he just got aggressive and insisted that it was his cow that was the mother of the calves. He shouted that today he would eat fresh meat unless the Court ruled in his favor.

Most of the animals were scared that the lion would start killing them. Many closed their mouths and said they were still thinking about a judgment that would be fair to both the lion and the hyena.

Others argued that it would be better to give the calves to the lion because the hyena had agreed to keep the lion's male cow. When the lion heard this, he said, "Yes, Yes, Yes, a good judgment is coming."

But some animals were whispering that the truth must be told. The hyena was right because the lion had only one cow, so how could that one male cow give birth. When the lion heard that, he said, "Now I am getting angry and tired of this Court." That made all the animals keep quiet.

Just then the Chief saw the rabbit with a bucket

of water on his head coming in a hurry to attend the Court. The Chief asked, "Mr. Rabbit, why are you late with an angry face?" Everyone in the Court kept quiet.

Mr. Rabbit replied, "Sir, Mr. Chief, forgive me, I was too busy caring for my father because he gave birth last night. I had to take water to him for his little baby."

When the lion heard Mr. Rabbit say this he shouted, "You stupid animal, how can your father who is a male give birth? It is only the female animal who can give birth. Why are you deceiving our Chief and the animal community?"

Mr. Rabbit replied to the lion, "Sir, if you know that, how could your male cow give birth to the twin calves? This means you are telling a great lie."

Everyone started to laugh. The Chief dismissed the case and awarded the calves to the hyena. "Let the lion take only his male cow. This is the judgment of the Court," said the Chief.

* * * * *

An important lesson of this story is that you must never try to cheat your neighbor

or anyone else, even if you are bigger and stronger. Another lesson is that justice will always prevail, as it did in this story. This may not happen right away. Sometimes we may have to be patient. But if we fight for justice, we will win in the end.

A TURTLE COMPETES
AGAINST TWO BIG ANIMALS

ONCE upon a time, Mr. Turtle would bring his children out of the river onto the land every morning. One day he saw that Mr. Elephant and Mr. Hippopotamus were eating by the river shore. The elephant was destroying tree branches and throwing them at the small animals. And the hippo was kicking rocks from the river onto the land with his powerful legs.

The small animals became afraid of the big animals and had to walk far away to find another grazing area where they could eat safely.

Mr. Elephant called out to Mr. Turtle, warning him not to be there because the area was for the big animals. "Small animals are without value," said Mr. Elephant. But Mr. Turtle told Mr. Elephant, "I am the strongest animal ever found in the water and on the land. If I want to move you from this area, I will."

The elephant replied, "Do you really mean that?" The turtle said, "I mean it." So they set a day for the competition to determine who was stronger. Before the appointed day, Mr. Turtle approached Mr. Hippopotamus, who had not heard about the competition.

"Mr. Hippo," said the turtle, "I am the strongest animal on the land. When I am on land I can pull you out of the water with a rope. That's how strong I am."

Mr. Hippo was a very good swimmer and did not like to leave the water. He knew he would suffer on land without the water to keep him cool in the hot sun. He also knew he was far stronger than Mr. Turtle. So he, too, agreed to a competition with Mr. Turtle, which the turtle then cleverly arranged to be at the same time as his challenge with Mr. Elephant.

When the day of the competition arrived, Mr. Elephant brought a big rope and gave it to the turtle to take into the water. The elephant said he would stay on the land and pull the turtle out of the water so that all the animals watching could laugh at him. Then the turtle would have to leave the area.

"We shall see about that, Mr. Elephant," said the turtle. "When I start to pull the rope, let us begin." With that, Mr. Turtle swam away with the rope. He went straight to Mr. Hippo, who believed he was the only one in the competition with Mr. Turtle that day.

Mr. Turtle handed the hippo the rope and said, just as he had told the elephant, "When I start to pull, let us begin." Mr. Hippo agreed. Then the turtle swam away and hid.

After a few minutes, the turtle pulled on the

rope from his hiding place. Feeling the tug, both big animals started to pull. The crowd began to cheer loudly. The big friends of the hippo all cheered him on against the turtle. They told the hippo to use all of his power to pull the turtle into the water so that they could laugh at him and chase him away forever.

At the same time, the big friends of the elephant cheered him on against the turtle. They told him to use all of his power to pull the turtle onto the land so that they could laugh at him and send him away forever.

The turtle also had many friends. All the reptiles in the water, who did not like the hippo, cheered for the turtle to pull the hippo onto the land. And all the small animals on the land were cheering for the turtle to pull the elephant into the water. The competition continued throughout the morning with fierce pulling by both the elephant and the hippo. Each thought he was fighting the turtle, and each was surprised not to be gaining any ground.

Meanwhile, during all the pulling, a mother rat and her children were caught in the middle of the competition. They were underground in their hole, and the rope was coming dangerously close. To protect her children, every time the rope passed over the opening to their hole, the mother rat bit it. Suddenly, around mid-day, the rope was cut into two parts.

When this happened, neither big animal felt any force. The hippo rose up out of the water. The elephant walked toward the shore. The elephant saw the hippo, and the hippo saw the elephant. Suddenly, both realized they were fighting each other and not the turtle. The crowd in the water and on the land also realized how each of the big animals had suffered at the hands of the turtle.

In the crowd was Ms. Frog, who lived both in the water and on the land. She told her children that it was good for these two big animals to fight without knowing who they were fighting. She said it was good because both big animals were scaring all the small animals.

Everything got quiet for many hours both in the water and on the land. The two big animals, who had always been friends, now understood that the huge fight had been for nothing. They had to admit that a clever turtle had outwitted them.

They then started to respect and value small animals. And this began an era when animals of all sizes grazed together and lived in peace.

* * * * *

This story teaches that you need to pay attention to your enemies and develop a plan to protect yourself. You must keep the plan secret from those who might hurt you, and remember that brainpower eventually triumphs over physical strength and size. If you do this, you may be able to establish peace, so everyone can live together in harmony.

Printed in the USA
CPSIA information can be obtained
at www.ICGtesting.com
LVHW051351210823
755829LV00003B/129

9 781532 095641